For my big brother

ARTIST'S NOTE
The illustrations were drawn on handmade paper using a black fine-liner
and then colored with watercolor paints.

Library of Congress Cataloging-in-Publication Data

Napp, Daniel, 1974–
Professor Bumble and the monster of the deep / by Daniel Napp.
p. cm.
Summary: When Professor Bumble and his goldfish Beluga come to their
favorite spot for their weekly swim, Otter warns them about a terrible
monster in the lake.
ISBN-13: 978-0-8109-9484-3 (hardcover)
ISBN-10: 0-8109-9484-4 (hardcover)
[1. Bears—Fiction. 2. Goldfish—Fiction. 3. Otters—Fiction. 4. Monsters—
Fiction.] I. Title.
PZ7.N153Pro 2008
[E]—dc22
2007016196

Book design by Maria Middleton

Printed and bound in China
10 9 8 7 6 5 4 3 2 1

HNA
harry n. abrams, inc.
a subsidiary of La Martinière Groupe

115 West 18th Street
New York, NY 10011
www.hnabooks.com

Daniel Napp

PROFESSOR BUMBLE
and the
MONSTER OF THE DEEP

Translated by
Hilary Schmitt-Thomas

Abrams Books for Young Readers
New York

Every Monday, Professor Bumble did the same thing . . .

He went swimming
with his friend Beluga.

But one day there was a stranger at their favorite spot.

"You can't go swimming here," said Otter as Professor Bumble put Beluga into the water. "You'll frighten away my fish."

"But we always go swimming here," bubbled Beluga.

"And none of the fish have ever complained," added Professor Bumble.

Otter angrily packed up his fishing gear. "Oh, all right then. But the Monster of the Deep will get you!"

"Monster of the Deep?" asked Professor Bumble.

"The Monster of the Deep lies in wait at the bottom of the lake!" said Otter. "It has three heads and five eyes. And a huge mouth with sharp teeth. It can swallow a bear in one bite!"

"Oh my!" said Professor Bumble.

Otter laughed, packed his things, and took off.

Beluga didn't want to waste any more time getting into the water.

"But what if the monster comes?" asked Professor Bumble.

"There's no such thing as the Monster of the Deep," bubbled Beluga.

Nevertheless, Professor Bumble preferred
to stay on land and keep an eye on his friend.
"Just to be on the safe side," he said.

Beluga slowly drifted out into the lake.
Suddenly his bowl tipped over and began to sink.
"Goodness gracious!" bubbled Beluga.

Professor Bumble watched helplessly as his friend
was pulled down into the depths.
"Oh no! The Monster of the Deep has got him!"
he cried.

"BELUGA, I'm coming!"

Could Professor Bumble save Beluga from the monster?

Professor Bumble jumped into the water and dived down. Deep, deep down.

In the darkness of the bottom of the lake, he found Beluga's bowl.

"BELUGA!"

cried Professor Bumble.

"Where?!" called Professor Bumble.
"Help!"
But Beluga had already attacked
the monster.

PLOFF!

PAFF!

PIFF!

Professor Bumble shot up like a rocket . . .

Meanwhile, Otter had found a quiet place to fish.
There was nobody there to disturb him.

He noticed some air bubbles on the surface
of the water.
A fish! Otter thought.
"It must be a big one!" he exclaimed excitedly.

But Monday was not over yet!

At home, Professor Bumble and Beluga hopped into the bathtub. It was not as big as the lake, but it did not have a monster in it. Nevertheless, Professor Bumble put on his water wings.

"Just to be on the safe side!" he said.